Enjoy this true story!

Sara W. Diamond

For my father, Robert Dewey Ward, who inspired this book, as well as my life. Thank you, Daddy, for all you taught me. You'll always be in my heart.

www.mascotbooks.com

Otter Joe Pete Finds a Home

For more information, please contact:
Mascot Books
560 Herndon Parkway #120
Herndon, VA 20170
info@mascotbooks.com

Library of Congress Control Number: 2016920254

CPSIA Code: PRT0117A
ISBN-13: 978-1-68401-118-6

Printed in the United States

Otter Joe Pete
FINDS A HOME

Written by Dr. Susan W. Diamond

Illustrated by Sarah Kate McGlenn

CHAPTER 1
GOING FISHING

It was the first day of summer break in Opp, Alabama, and nine-year-old Bobby was getting ready to do his favorite thing in the whole wide world: fishing! The river ran about a hundred yards or so behind their house, so Bobby didn't have to go far. But first, he headed over to the worm bed he and Daddy had made to dig up some fresh bait.

It only took a few minutes of digging around in the leaves, vegetable and fruit scraps, and of course, plenty of good old fashioned dirt, before Bobby had a can full of squiggly, wiggly earthworms (and some pretty filthy fingernails)! But a little dirt never hurt anybody, so Bobby wiped his hands on his pants and went to the river.

Was today the day he was going to catch some bream or maybe even a catfish or two?

His mouth watered as he thought about Mama frying up fish, hushpuppies, and homemade French fries for supper! Daddy would be so proud if he came home from a long day of crushing hay in the fields, only to find Bobby had caught dinner. Bobby wanted to provide for the family too!

But as it turned out, Bobby didn't catch a single fish that day. He didn't even put one squiggly, wiggly worm on a hook! Instead, he made an exciting discovery that would change everything...

Chapter 2
Skipping Stones

When Bobby got to his favorite fishing spot, he set down his pole and worm can. Then he noticed a few smooth rocks nearby. "I know!" he said. "I'll skip them like Daddy showed me." He picked up two smooth stones and flicked the first one. *One...two...three* skips and the stone disappeared into the river.

"I can do better than that!" Bobby said, frowning. He took the other stone in his hand, and with great focus, he flicked his wrist just right. *One...two...three...four* skips before the rock *ker-plunked* into the stream.

"Can I get to five?" Bobby wondered aloud. "I bet I can... but I've got to find the perfect stone for the job." And so, he slowly searched along the riverbank for just the right rock.

The sunshine glistened against the stones on the riverbank, and Bobby thought they looked like glittering diamonds! There were hundreds, maybe even thousands of stones lining the riverbank around him.

Then, Bobby saw something move...

CHAPTER 3
AN ANIMAL FOUND

"What is that?" he said, squinting so he could see more clearly. It was no bigger than his hand and it blended in with the color of the riverbank. But it was moving—it was alive!

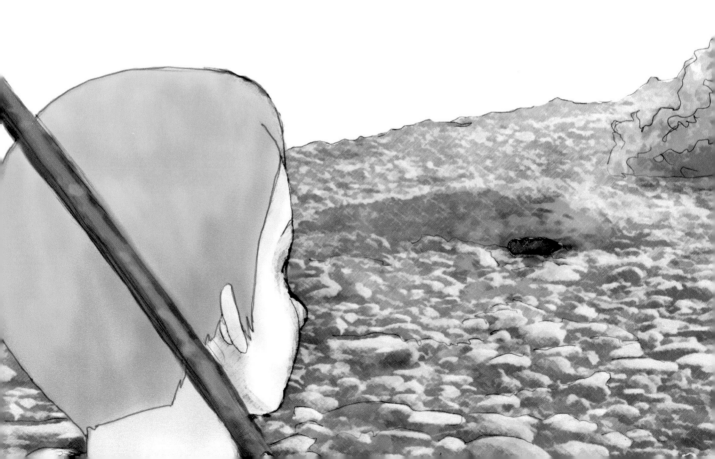

Bobby bent down on his knees to get a closer look. The little animal was lying on his back, like he was sunbathing. He had four short, webbed feet, two tiny ears, two black-button eyes, a triangle of a nose...and a long tail! Bobby had never seen anything like it before!

But what was he doing out here all alone? Bobby looked around. There was no nest, no Mommy or Daddy, no brothers or sisters, and no one to take care of him and keep him safe. A chill ran down Bobby's spine. He knew what he had to do.

Carefully, he scooped the little baby critter up in his hands and gently placed him in his bib pocket. He carried his bait can and cane pole with his left hand, and kept the other close to his heart where the baby whatever-it-was was safe and secure. When Bobby got home, he called out to his mother from the back porch door, "Hey Mama, come look what I found."

CHAPTER 4
THAT'S AN OTTER

"Well, I declare," Mama said. "Bobby, that's an otter!"

"What's an otter?" Bobby asked.

"It's an animal that lives near the river," Mama explained. "They love to play in the water, but what are you doing with this one in your pocket?"

"He was all alone," Bobby said, "and he's just a baby. I couldn't leave him."

Mama raised an eyebrow. "He's a pup is what he is," she said. "That's what baby otters are called. You sure you didn't see any other otters nearby?"

"No, ma'am," Bobby said. "This little pup was all by himself, and I was worried about what would happen to him, so I brought him home."

"That's a very kind thing for you to do, Bobby," Mama said. "But taking care of an animal—especially a baby—is a big responsibility. And I don't know if you're old enough to take care of him. Feeding and cleaning and making sure he has everything he needs is a lot for a nine-year-old boy to do."

"Oh Mama, I can do it! I know I can!" Bobby exclaimed.

"Well, let's see what Daddy says when he gets home, okay? In the meantime, I think this little fella might be hungry. Bring him on inside."

Mama went into the kitchen and poured some milk into a bowl. "Grown-up otters eat fish, but this little pup is too small for that," she explained. "Pass him here, Bobby, and we'll get him fed."

Mama gently wrapped a dishtowel around the pup, cradling him in her left arm. Then, she took a piece of bread and dipped it into the bowl of milk. When she brought the milk-soaked bread to the mouth of the little otter, he hungrily sucked the milk right out of the bread!

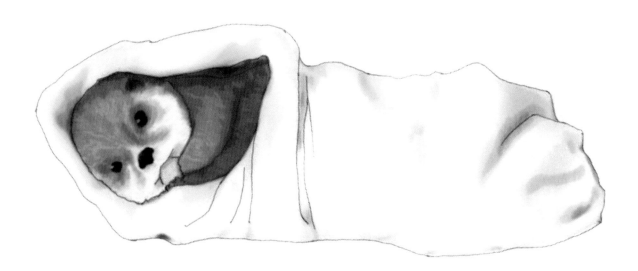

Before long, the pup's tummy was full and he was fast asleep. "Now that we've got him fed, where do you think this little fella should stay?" Mama asked. "That's the second most important thing of taking care of an animal."

"Can he sleep with me?" Bobby asked excitedly.

Mama shook her head. "He needs a space of his own right now."

Bobby frowned. But it wasn't long before an idea popped into his head. "I know!" he said, grinning, and he took off to the shed.

He came back with a sturdy cardboard box. Next, he took some old newspaper and tore it into shreds for the lining. And finally, he announced that the towel Mama wrapped him in would be his blanket.

"Great work, Bobby," said Mama. "Let's keep him on the back porch for now. When Daddy gets home we'll decide what to do from there."

Bobby could hardly wait!

CHAPTER 6
WHAT'S AN OTTER?

Bobby sat on the porch watching the little pup sleep peacefully. Suddenly, Bobby heard a loud yawn behind him. It was his five-year-old sister, Alice! She had just woken up from her nap.

"What's that?" Alice asked, peeking over Bobby's shoulder into the box.

"It's a pup. Shhh, he's sleeping," Bobby answered.

"That doesn't look like a puppy."

"It's not a dog puppy...it's an otter puppy," Bobby said.

"An utter puppy?" little Alice asked.

"No...an otter puppy!" Bobby laughed.

"What's an otter?"

"It's an animal that lives near the river and plays in the water. He was all alone by the riverbank, so I brought him home with me. Look!" Bobby said. "He's waking up!"

The little otter yawned and stretched his tiny webbed feet.

"Ohhh...he's sooo cute!" Alice exclaimed. "Are we going to keep him?"

"I hope so," said Bobby. "But Daddy has to say it's okay."

"Oh, I hope he does!" Alice said.

CHAPTER 7
WHAT'S IN A NAME?

"What are we going to call him?" asked Alice. "Can we call him Baby?"

Bobby rolled his eyes. "He won't always be a baby, Alice. He needs a real name."

"What about Alice?" she said, smiling widely.

"But he's a boy otter! And that's your name," said Bobby. "It can't be Alice."

Alice thought for a minute. "What about Joe? We can name him after Uncle Joe, like how you're named after Daddy."

"My middle name comes from Daddy," Bobby reminded her.

"Okay then, we can give him a middle name too," said Alice. "What goes with Joe?"

Bobby and Alice were quiet for a minute, and then Bobby said, "I know, I know! Why don't we call him Joe Pete? Pete after my best friend. He'll like that. Let's go tell Mama!"

They found Mama in the kitchen, frying chicken for supper.

"Mama," Alice said, "Guess what? We named the otter puppy!"

"You did?" asked Mama. "Well, what is it, what's his name?"

"Joe Pete!" they cried together.

"Joe Pete..." considered Mama. "Why, that's a really fine name."

Alice went on, "I came up with Joe, for Uncle Joe, and Bobby came up with Pete, for Pete down the street!"

But then Bobby realized something. "Uncle Joe and Pete are great and have great names, but I want this little pup to have his own special name."

"I believe you're onto something there, Bobby," said Mama. "Each one of us—even this little pup—is unique, created and loved by God. It's important for us to remember that. Let me think…" said Mama. "What about calling him Otter Joe Pete? No one else in the whole wide world has that name!"

Bobby and Alice both laughed at the same time. And at the sound of his new name, the little pup joyfully patted his front paws on his belly.

"Look at Otter Joe Pete!" giggled Alice. "He's clapping for his new name! It's perfect."

Bobby and Alice spent the rest of the afternoon with Otter Joe Pete, feeding him more milk-soaked bread and watching him sleep as they took turns holding him. Otter Joe Pete looked so peaceful and happy. They hoped and prayed that Daddy would let him stay.

CHAPTER 8

A little later that afternoon, Bobby heard the familiar sound of Daddy's Diamond T truck coming down the dirt road that led to the house. Bobby's heart began to race. What would Daddy say? What if he said no? What would happen to Otter Joe Pete?

The back porch screen door swung open, and Daddy's eyes fell on his two children sitting by a box on the floor. "Hey kids! What have you got there?"

Without delay, Alice shouted out with unbridled joy, "We've got Otter Joe Pete!"

Bobby, knowing that Daddy would need more of an explanation, quickly told how he found the pup by the riverbank all alone, and that he was concerned for his safety.

He told Daddy about feeding Otter Joe Pete, putting a box together for his bed, and how he would take care of him if Daddy would give him the chance.

Everything was very quiet for a moment. Then Daddy said, "Let's go down to the river and make sure Otter Joe Pete's family isn't looking for him. We wouldn't want his mom to be sad and scared about losing her baby."

Bobby grimaced. He hadn't thought about that.

He led Daddy to the exact place where he found Otter Joe Pete. After looking around, they found a den, but no one was there. A few steps away, they came upon a very sad sight. There, lying under a big oak tree, they saw the lifeless remains of an adult otter. It appeared that another animal had attacked it, and it had died.

"I think this was Otter Joe Pete's mother," Daddy said quietly.

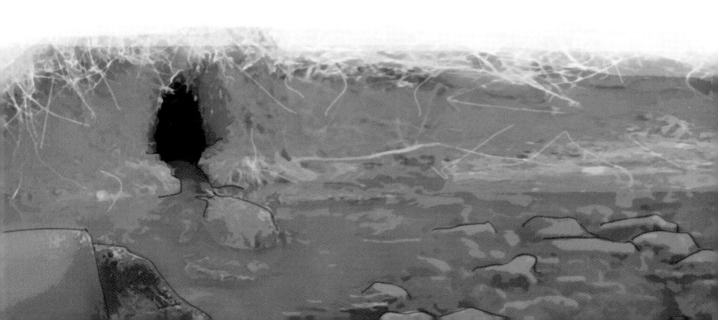

Tears welled up in Bobby's eyes. What would he do if he lost one of his parents? It was so unfair. Poor Otter Joe Pete.

Daddy put his arm around Bobby's shoulder. "Sometimes bad things happen, Bobby," he said. "But when bad things happen, we have a choice about how we can respond to them. We can do nothing but get sad or mad, or we can do something to make it better. You did something to make it better for Otter Joe Pete, son. And I'm proud of you for being so kind to someone in need."

"So," he continued, "to answer your question...yes, you can keep him!"

"Yay!" Bobby shouted as his tears turned into tears of joy. He gave Daddy the biggest hug he could, crying, "Thank you, Daddy! Thank you!"

As soon as they got home, Bobby shared the good news with Alice and Mama. But he didn't tell Alice about Otter Joe Pete's Mommy; she was just too little for that.

And that was the day that kindness and love made the way for a little baby otter to survive, receive a name, and find a loving home and family.

And so began the adventures of Otter Joe Pete!

BEYOND THE STORY...
THINGS YOU "OTTER" DISCUSS

The following are some questions based on themes that adults and children can talk about together.

1. When Bobby found Otter Joe Pete all alone on the riverbank, he took him home so he would be safe. This was a great act of kindness. What does the word "kind" mean to you? What are some ways that you can be kind to others?

2. When Bobby asked Mama if he could keep Otter Joe Pete, she wondered if Bobby was old enough to take on the responsibility of caring for him. Taking responsibility means that you can be depended on to take care of something that you have promised to do. What are some of your responsibilities? Can you name something that you can be depended upon to do in your family?

3. Together, Bobby, Alice, and Mama come up with a very distinct name: Otter Joe Pete. As Mama said, "Everyone is unique, created and loved by God." Where did your name come from? Were you named after a relative or friend? Do you know what your name means?

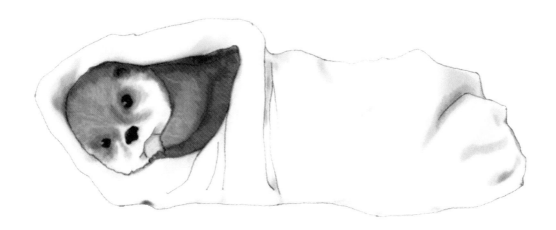

4. There is a sad note to this story, as we learn that Otter Joe Pete's mother has died. Bobby experiences compassion, which means to care for someone who is in pain. Have you ever had compassion for someone who was hurting? When did that happen? How did you feel? What did you do?

5. Bobby is reminded by his father that we have a choice about what to do when bad things happen: we can be sad or angry, or we can choose to do something to make things better. Can you think of a time when you had to make a choice about what to do when something bad happened? What did you do? Could a different choice have been made? If so, what might have happened if you had made that choice?

About The Book

Otter Joe Pete Finds a Home is based on the true story of the author's father, who, as a little boy from southern rural Alabama, found an orphaned otter pup by the riverbank who became his pet and best friend. Susan grew up hearing stories about the adventures (and misadventures) of little Bobby and Otter Joe Pete by her grandmother, Onnie V. Ward, one of the world's greatest storytellers!

Bob Ward died in 1982 from lung cancer when Susan and her sisters were in their early 20s. As they married and their families grew, the story of Otter Joe Pete was shared, along with many other stories about their grandfather. Now, as great-grandchildren are coming into the family, Susan felt it was time to write the story and share it not only with them, but with children everywhere who love a great story.

A family project, Susan is joined by her niece, Sarah Kate McGlenn, as illustrator. Sarah received her BA from Flagler College in Art Education in 2012 and is a freelance artist. The beautiful artwork in this book reflects both Sarah's talent as well as her love for a grandfather she never knew, except from stories like this one.

ABOUT THE AUTHOR

Rev. Dr. Susan Ward Diamond is Senior Minister of Florence Christian Church (Disciples of Christ) in Florence, Kentucky. She has served churches in Kentucky, Alabama, and Florida since her ordination in 1990.

Susan has been married to Ron L. Diamond, professional magician, stage hypnotist, and motivational speaker since 1979. They are the proud parents of their four-legged daughters, dachshunds Sweet Pea and Bella.

In addition to *Otter Joe Pete Finds a Home*, Susan is author of *The Daily Grind: God With Your Coffee*, a book of devotional observations about life and faith. She has written for several magazines and has a blog entitled, "Pastor Susan's Thought for the Day."

Have a book idea?
Contact us at:

info@mascotbooks.com | www.mascotbooks.com